BOOK 2
CHASE THE MOLE

WRITTEN BY
KIRSTY HOLMES

BookLife
PUBLISHING

©2023 **BookLife Publishing Ltd.**
King's Lynn, Norfolk, PE30 4LS, UK

ISBN 978-1-80505-362-0

All rights reserved. Printed in China.
A catalogue record for this book is
available from the British Library.

Agent of RADAR: Chase the Mole
Written by Kirsty Holmes
Based on a story by Robin Twiddy
Edited by Robin Twiddy
Illustrated by Kel Winser

ABOUT THE AUTHORS

When she was little, Kirsty knew everything. When it became clear she didn't, she started reading books. Eventually, she realised she would never know everything, and started making things up instead, which is much more fun. Today, she lives mostly in her imagination and hopes you like this story as much as she liked writing it, which is a lot.

Robin has always loved stories. As a child, he would often be found daydreaming, lost in yet another tale in his head. As an adult, he has had the great privilege of taking those stories in his head and sharing them with children all around the world. Robin lives with his partner and their two young girls, who have proven to be a wellspring of joy and inspiration for him.

ABOUT THE ILLUSTRATOR

Kel has been drawing cartoons, superheroes and comics for as long as he can remember. He divides his time between teaching the next generation of cartoonists, making illustrations and comics for himself and publishers, spending time with his family, and growing an enormous beard! Kel lives in Norwich, UK with his wife and son.

MISSION LOG
OCT347-X ("ZERO")

Entry 0974-i4849-C

Record Type: New Recruit

Recruit Name: Chase, Nathan

Recruit Age: 13 years 7 months

Recruited by: Agent Jack Masters

Reporting to: Commander A. C. Foxley

Reason for Recruitment:

During a mission to stop RUIN firing the Storm Cannon and destroying the world, Agent Jack Masters was chased by RUIN agents into a local laser tag centre. Inside, he met local schoolboy Nathan Chase.

Chase was able to get the super-intelligent and essential A.I. OCT347-X, known as Zero (me), out of the laser tag centre and across town. En route to Saint's Hill, the highest point in town, Chase ably fought off RUIN agents and a growing storm and was able to get the A.I. to Commander Foxley in time. The RUIN plan was foiled, and the Storm Cannon was stopped.

Mission: **SUCCESS**

Deep Cover Details:

Agent Chase will attend his usual civilian school during the week, where he will continue to attempt to blend in. He is showing... variable success. Chase attends RADAR Academy on Saturday mornings. He will attempt not to rouse the suspicion of his mother, who believes he is at laser tag.

Training Notes:

Agent Chase shows considerable promise. He is taking to training well and is very... enthusiastic. Agent Masters is pleased with his progress, but Commander Foxley is unsure if Chase is ready for a tougher challenge in the field.

Mission Status:

The Storm Cannon was destroyed by my brilliant virus (if I do say so myself). Several ninjas were captured by Agent Masters during the storm, but they refuse to talk.

RUIN remains active...

Zero: OUT

CHAPTER ONE
THE BASIC LASER EVASION PROTOCOL

Nathan Chase raced along the cold, grey corridor, the distant 'pew, pew' of laser guns growing louder behind him. His heart pounded. His chest heaved. Still, he pushed harder, urging himself on despite the ache in his legs. On his wrist, a device that looked a little  like a watch, but obviously much cooler, vibrated sharply.

"Remember your training, sir," the device said.

The lasers were getting closer.

PEW! PEW! PEW!

Nathan swung around another corner.

"Erm... Remind me, Zero?" He jiggled his wrist a little. The device let out a little sigh.

"The Basic Laser Evasion Protocol, sir. One: make random movements." Nathan tumbled to the right as the first laser shots flew past, then rolled quickly to the left. "Two: be unpredictable." A pair of ninjas rounded the corner in hot pursuit of RADAR's latest recruit. Nathan made to jump, then fell to the floor as all three fired high, aiming for where his head would have been. "Very good, sir. Didn't see that coming. And three – WOAH!" The AI vibrated as Nathan suddenly sprinted forward. "MOST IMPORTANTLY, sir, three: **KEEP YOUR COOL.**"

"Got it. Random, unpredictable..." He rolled up his sleeve, pointing a fist at the ninjas. "And COOL." He fired a blast from the device on his wrist. Two ninjas, dressed in green, froze to the spot. Nathan thumbed his nose as he ran past

them, on down the corridor...

...and skidded to a halt just in time. The corridor ended in a huge drop.

"OK. Zero. Situation, erm... bad. How deep is the drop?" Nathan didn't want to know.

"You don't want to know, sir," said Zero.

"And how far is the jump?" Nathan squinted. It looked do-able, with a bit of a run-up.

"Six metres, sir." A whole section of the bridge was missing.

"Can I make it with the nano-grapple?" Nathan said.

"No, sir. With your best jump-and-swing you have only ever managed a personal best of five metres and sixty-three centimetres. You would be thirty-seven centimetres short, sir. Prediction: failure."

Nathan reconsidered his options. He could hear footsteps echoing in the corridor behind him.

They were getting closer. No time to think. Time to **ACT!**

"Get the nano-bots ready." Nathan crouched, eyes on the other side. Behind him, he heard laser fire.

"Sir? What is the *plan*, sir?"

Nathan sprinted forwards. As he leapt into the air he shouted: "Zero: NANO-STEP!"

"I see," said Zero. "No plan. Very good, sir."

Zero released a stream of orange nano-bots that formed into a mid-air step. Nathan's foot connected with the step, and he thrust his arm forwards again.

"Zero: NANO-GRAPPLE!" he cried. "Wait – what?"

Beneath his foot, as he pushed down to leap-and-swing, the step was melting away! The cloud of bots moved upwards to form the grappling hook, dissolving the step beneath him. For a moment, Nathan hung in the air, not quite on the step, grasping at the misty, half-formed nano-grapple... and

plummeted into the massive drop below.

"Oof!" he said, as he hit the training room floor a moment later. The hologram of the corridor

– and, thankfully, the drop – disappeared. The familiar green-and-black grid of the Simnasium training centre returned. Nathan rubbed his knee. A familiar voice behind reminded him of his hurt pride.

"What went wrong there, Kid?" Jack Masters, super-suave super-spy, stepped across the training floor.

"What went wrong there," said Zero, "was leaving me out of the plan."

"There wasn't time to plan!" said Nathan. "There were ninjas, remember?"

"Holo-ninjas," replied Zero. "If you had told me the plan, I could have told you I couldn't do it. Instead, we fell nineteen hundred and fifty-three metres and by my calculation, I would have been…"

"Alright, Zero. That's why we train here, in the Simnasium. Because while we are learning, we mess up," said Jack. "What did I say, Kid: jump…?"

"…Then shoot," Nathan groaned.

"So, tell me what went wrong." Jack Masters tapped his tablet screen.

Nathan hesitated. It should have worked.

"May I make a suggestion, sir?" Zero vibrated on Nathan's wrist. "Error 2537-19B?"

Nathan had no idea what that meant. "Sorry, Zero – what is Error 25… what you just said?"

"A shortage of nano-bots caused a malfunction in – "

"Not enough nano-bots." Nathan interrupted, and flopped onto his back. Obviously.

"Zero has a limited supply of nano-bots, Nathan. You can't make two things at once," said Jack, tapping into the tablet again. "They don't call Zero artificial intelligence for nothing. Don't worry, Kid. You're training. The trouble with training is, you don't know what you don't know."

Nathan rubbed his knee. "Until you find out."

Jack nodded. "And you found out. So, you fell. So what? What did you learn?"

"Jump... THEN shoot," Nathan said. "Do I get a gold star now?" He smiled at Jack.

"No," said Jack, helping him up. "Not this time, kid. Off to your next class."

CHAPTER TWO
THE FUTURE OF RADAR

He wore only black. He moved silently. And he *hated* sloppy handwriting. Rumours swirled around the academy – nothing confirmed, though. Some said he was raised by warrior nuns. Others claimed he was hundreds of years old. No one seemed to know anything for sure about him at all. None of it sounded believable, anyway. Agent Blackthorn was the most feared – and most mysterious – agent of RADAR. He was also the history teacher.

And today he was *really* disappointed with the latest recruits.

Blackthorn stalked up and down the classroom, slamming assignments onto the desks of the RADAR recruits. Nathan's assignment had a LOT of red lines on it. Blackthorn's eyes were narrow. His voice was low. Nathan would almost have preferred it if he had been shouting. Blackthorn moved around the room, growling low like a hungry wolf.

"So," he said, pacing across the floor in front of the students. "This is it. The future of RADAR, sitting here before me." He stopped, his heels coming together with a little click. "I suppose you are all very pleased with yourselves." He smiled the least happy smile Nathan had ever seen.

Nathan glanced around the classroom. Between regular school and being a secret agent there hadn't been much time for social stuff. He didn't know the other students of RADAR

Academy very well yet. To his right, a Black girl with fiery orange hair pushed her big round glasses up her nose with a shaky finger. She stared down at the open laptop in front of her and typed, avoiding the eye of the prowling teacher.

Blackthorn crossed the room to her. She froze, hands still on the keyboard. She didn't look up, but behind her huge glasses her eyes widened.

"Am I interrupting you, Recruit?" Blackthorn's voice was so low and quiet that Nathan had to strain to hear.

"N... n... no, sir," said the girl, quietly. Blackthorn leaned down until he was level with her face.

"THEN WHY THE INCESSANT TAPPING?" he screamed. He slammed the laptop lid closed, just missing the girl's fingers as she whisked them back.

"For over a hundred years, RADAR has stood against the chaos and destruction of RUIN. One hundred years! And to carry on the fight they send me, what? YOU? This one," he gestured at the trembling girl, "only talks to these machines. This one," he carried on, whirling round to face a tall, fair-haired boy in a martial arts uniform. "Only SEVEN black belts. Pah!"

The boy, twirling a silver throwing star between his fingers, opened his mouth to protest that seven black belts was quite a lot for a thirteen-year-old, but before he could speak, Blackthorn had plucked the star from his fingers and wedged it precisely between the boy's teeth. The teacher was a blur of black robes. Nathan had never seen anyone move so fast.

"Oi!" the boy said in surprise. "**Aii Oh Eeeee arrrrre!**"

Blackthorn turned his attention to Nathan.

"And *then*," he said, "Jack Masters turns up with... this." Blackthorn gestured at Nathan as if Jack had left a heap of stinky laundry in his classroom. "I am supposed to train this to face the Baron! It makes me want to weep." He grasped Nathan by the wrist. "And this thing." He said, inspecting Zero like an unpleasant growth on Nathan's arm. "Make sure your watch is set on *silent*."

Zero vibrated.

"I am not a watch. I am oC — oof!"

Nathan slapped his palm across Zero's face, then pulled his hoodie sleeve over his hand. He grinned up at Blackthorn. Blackthorn did not smile back.

"Can you even tell me what RADAR stands for?" He sounded very much like he did not expect Nathan to be able to do so. Well, Nathan would show him.

"RADAR. Yes. It stands for Rebel Agents… Doing…. All the…" He trailed off. Blackthorn's eyebrows knitted together above his eyes like two spiders having a fight.

"Rebel Agents Defending Against Ruin!" rang out a voice from the front of the class.

The pale girl in the front row had black fingernails. Her black hair shone in the classroom lighting. She sat primly in her chair, a slight smile

 on her cool black lips. She looked like she was not afraid of Blackthorn *at all*. Nathan's stomach flip-flopped. This girl was *really* confident.

"Oh. We have a volunteer," Blackthorn sneered, turning on the girl. She smiled wider. "And I suppose you also know what RUIN stands for, Recruit?"

"Ruin Unleashed by International Nobodies." She didn't miss a beat. Better still, Blackthorn had grown tired of Nathan and was focussing his attention on her. And she seemed to be loving it.

"What about the B—" Blackthorn began but this time the girl interrupted him.

"Baron von Thustra runs RUIN. He is..." She

lowered her voice as if revealing a secret. "The bad guy." The Black girl giggled. The blond boy spat the throwing star out and it landed in the wall. Nathan couldn't take his eyes off the pale girl.

"The agents of RUIN could be anywhere. That's why they are called Nobodies. They could be *anybody*..." She stood up.

Nathan realised his mouth was open. This was amazing...

"And he wants—" Blackthorn said...

"—only one thing," said the girl. "To RULE THE WORRRRRLLLLD!" She threw her hands above her head, cackling wildly. Blackthorn looked like he was going to pop.

Nathan laughed. "Brilliant!"

She smiled directly at him and winked. Nathan grinned back. He felt his cheeks flush –

THWACK!

Blackthorn blurred again and this time the throwing star was out of the wall and embedded in

Nathan's desk before he'd had a chance to blush. Nathan fell backwards, crashing to the floor.

"Detention! Do you hear me?" Blackthorn pointed directly at Nathan. Behind him, the girl kicked her feet up onto the desk. "I said **DETENTION.** How dare you laugh at this? RUIN is not a joke! You may have been handpicked by Jack Masters but I have no idea why. RUIN have agents on every street corner and THIS is what they send me to defend RADAR? **JOKES?!**"

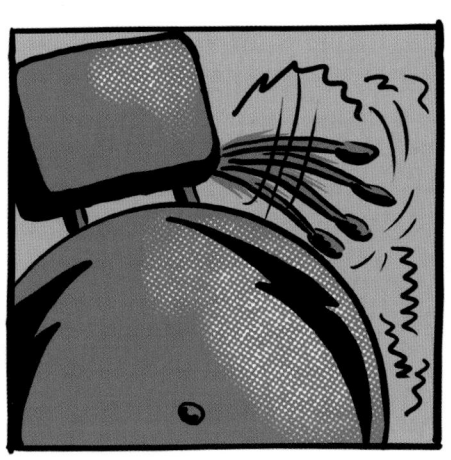

BRRRRIIING!!

Saved by the bell, thought Nathan as they all scraped their chairs back and stood.

"GET OUT!" screamed Blackthorn. **"GET OUT, ALL OF YOU!"**

CHAPTER THREE
THE REASON WE'RE HERE

Having lessons at RADAR HQ was cool, Nathan had to admit. As they scrambled into the corridor, Nathan had to dodge and swerve to avoid busy agents on important missions rushing back and forth. He caught up to the boy in the martial arts uniform. He was tall, so easy to spot.

"Hey," he said, drawing up next to the boy. "Do you really have seven black belts?"

"Yeah," said the boy. He frowned at Nathan, raising a hand sharply. "Want me to show you how I got 'em?"

The Black girl joined the conversation. "Only seven, Kicks? Is that all?" she teased.

"Well how many have YOU got, Screens?" pouted Kicks, dropping his hand.

"I don't need a black belt," said the girl. "I've got all the butt-kicking power I need right here." She tapped the cover of her laptop.

"How many RUIN ninjas are you going to defeat with that?" Kicks snorted.

"All of them, if I lock the whole building down with a few clicks of the keys," retorted Screens. "Or… I could change all your martial arts grades to big fat Fs."

"Agent Smiler said you're not allowed to do that again." Kicks scowled at her.

A group of RADAR agents ran through the group, nudging Nathan into Kicks. "Hey, watch it, Chase," Kicks spat at him. "At least Blackthorn can see what Jack Masters can't. You don't belong here."

The words stung Nathan.

"What do you mean?" he asked.

Kicks laughed. "You don't fight. You don't code. You don't seem that smart. Why are you here?"

"It's a good question," said Screens. "We were all personally chosen because we excel at something. I have three PhDs in computing, and Kicks is working on his eighth black belt. What's your skill?"

Nathan opened and closed his mouth. Nothing came out. He didn't know. He could hardly boast to these amazing super-kids that he'd never taken a hit at Laser Tag. Could he?

"Erm… I saved the world?" he offered. That had to count for something.

"Any one of us could have done that," scoffed Kicks. "Probably faster, too. Especially if we had that fancy high-tech watch doing all the work."

Zero, on Nathan's wrist, coughed.

"I am NOT a watch. I am 0CT347-X. You can call me Zero."

Zara arrived, nudging Kicks slightly so he stumbled. She smiled at Nathan.

"We're all here for a reason, Kicks. Nathan has his. I have mine. And they…" She linked arms with Nathan. "Are none of your business."

Just then, the corridor fell silent. Every agent turned and saluted the group of top agents who were bustling down the corridor. At the head of the group, Commander Foxley looked very serious. Behind him, the most senior agents of RADAR were talking urgently in low, hushed voices.

Foxley led the group past the recruits. As they passed, Jack Masters reached over and gave Nathan a fist bump. He spoke quickly behind his hand.

"Don't worry – important RUIN intel has

just come in. We got this, Kid." He hurried away, following Foxley and the other senior agents into the Briefing Room. The heavy door slammed closed, locking the top agents into the highest security room in the building. The Briefing Room was a fortress. Walls

a metre thick. A door so heavy it took three people to open it. The room had its own ventilation, temperature control, and security system. It was right in the heart of RADAR HQ. And Foxley was in there with all his top agents?

Something **BIG** was going on.

CHAPTER FOUR
THE PROBLEM IS AMONG US

Kicks pressed his face up to the briefing room door.

"I can't hear anything!" he grumbled.

Zara's eyes rolled. "I think that's the point?" she said. "It wouldn't be a secure briefing room if RUIN could just listen at the door, would it?" She dragged them all into a neighbouring classroom.

"But I wanna know what's going on." Kicks was whining again. "Screeeeeens?"

Screens played innocent. "Yes?"

"Can you hack into the security system so we can listen?"

"Of course I can," said Screens.

"YES!" shouted Kicks.

"I won't, obviously." Screens pushed her glasses up her nose. "But I CAN."

"Pleeeeeeease?" begged Kicks. "I just want to listen!"

"Nope." The girl stood firm. "I will get detention forever if I get caught hacking RADAR systems again."

"Don't worry, Screens. We know it can't be hacked. Just say you can't do it," said Zara. "We're all friends here, right?"

"I can do it!" Screens bristled. She opened

her laptop. "Look. It's easy. You just..." She pressed a few buttons and a grainy picture of the briefing room appeared on the screen. "Obviously."

They crowded around the laptop as Screens, sighing a little, fiddled with the settings. The picture swam in and out of focus.

"I can't hear it." Kicks was complaining again.

"Hang on..." said Screens, tapping furiously. "Something seems to be... interfering... No, got it."

Foxley's voice crackled from the laptop's little speakers.

"...thing is, agents, we have a problem," said Foxley. He paced the room. "A major problem."

"What is it, Arthur?" said Jack Masters. Nathan didn't even know Commander Foxley HAD a first name. He leaned in. He was right next to Zara. She smelled like cinnamon. Nathan realised his palms were sweaty. Must be the excitement, he thought.

"Where's Blackthorn?" Zara muttered. He looked at the screen. She was right. Why wasn't Blackthorn in the meeting?

"You don't think he's the mole?" Nathan asked?

"Shh." said Zara, pointing to the screen.

Foxley leaned over the table.

"Agents, I hate to tell you that this time, the problem is among us. RADAR has... **a MOLE!**"

"Eugh," said Kicks. "I hate rodents."

Zara audibly sighed. "A mole is a spy, Kicks. RADAR has a spy."

Kicks frowned. "Obviously." He spoke slowly, as if Zara wasn't understanding him. "WE. ARE. ALL. SPIES."

Zara took a short breath, opened her mouth, then changed her mind. Nathan stepped in.

"A mole is a spy sent to spy on other spies, Kicks. Someone from RUIN is working at RADAR!"

"Who?" Kicks jumped into a fighting stance, hands out, ready to chop some bad guys. "Where?"

"Stand down, Kicks. The RUIN agent's not in here," said Screens. "Shh!"

On screen, the agents were looking at each other, shocked. Agent Smiler was shaking his head. Foxley spread some papers out on the table.

"We don't know who the mole is. But we do know what they want. The List," he said.

The agents' gasps could be clearly heard over

the intercom.

"What's The List?" said Nathan.

"Oh, NO." Screens had gone pale, her cheeks ashen. "The List is a top-secret database. It has the names and real identities of all our field agents. If RUIN got hold of that…"

"Disaster," said Zara. "It would mean disaster for RADAR – and victory for RUIN."

They looked at each other in shock. Zara broke the silence.

"What are they saying now?" she said. "Do they know who it is?"

Foxley was now sitting at the table with the agents. They were talking over the papers. Their voices were hard to make out. Screens turned up the volume and they all leaned in.

"So, we all agree," Foxley crackled. "The mole MUST BE.... **COUGH COUGH!**"

On screen, the room filled with bright smoke! All the agents coughed, trying to protect their heads with their jackets. Behind Jack Masters, an air vent popped from the wall.

"Oh no!" cried Nathan. "RUIN!"

One by one, three RUIN ninjas dropped through the vent into the briefing room.

Alarms screamed through the corridors. **THUNK! THUNK!** Heavy metal shutters fell across the doors. Lights flashed.

"What's going on?" shouted Nathan over the noise. "Why aren't we being affected by the gas?"

"Lockdown!" Zara replied, fingers in her ears. "Looks like a Category Three Alert."

"You're welcome!" yelled Screens.

"Can you kill the alarms?" shouted Kicks. Screens tapped; the alarms fell silent.

"Now what?" Screens said. "I've got control of the whole building."

"If those ninjas – or Blackthorn – are after The List, they'll be heading for the Central Server Room," said Screens. "That's where it's kept."

"How would they get it out?" asked Zara.

"On a memory stick," said Screens. "Old technology that can't be hacked. Like these." She showed off a keyring on which a rainbow of coloured USB memory sticks clattered. "They can download it onto one of these and go. Retro, but reliable."

"Let's go!" shouted Kicks, ready for a fight. Nathan looked at Zara. She smiled at him again. Nathan liked it when she did. Zara was clever, clear-headed and cool. He felt like they were becoming friends.

"Screens?" said Zara, turning away. "Can you sort out a route to the Central Server Room from here?"

"Obviously." Screens was already typing.

CHAPTER FIVE
THE PLAN GOES EXACTLY TO PLAN

The four recruits scrambled quietly along the corridor. Screens, her laptop strapped to her front like a mobile tech lab, tapped and double-clicked, and around them locks sprang open and doors slid closed. Screens' eyes didn't leave her digital map. The Central Server Room was marked with a flashing star.

"Screens," said Zara, as they came to a stop. "Those memory sticks of yours?"

Screens jangled the plastic sticks on her multi-coloured keyring. "Yes? Some of these are vintage, you know. 1990's technology."

Zara smiled. "What do you say we put them

to good use? Can you make a dummy version of The List? It doesn't have to fool anyone for long. It just needs to look good at a glance."

"Obviously," said Screens, already tapping.

"Great," said Zara. "When you're done, put it on one of the memory sticks."

"What's the plan, Zara?" asked Nathan. Zara winked.

"When we get into the server room, I'll save the fake database from the stick to the system. When RUIN get here, they'll steal the fake and…" She whistled. "Off they go!"

"Shh!" Screens closed the laptop and herded them all backwards. "Look!"

Blackthorn rounded the corner.

"How did he get through my security hack?" muttered Screens.

"More importantly – what's he doing here?" said Nathan.

Blackthorn stopped by the armoury, looking from side to side before entering. Nathan, finger to his lips, gestured to the others to stay where they were, and crept after him.

Inside, he hunched into the shadows. Blackthorn was muttering to himself in a language Nathan didn't know. He opened locker after locker of weapons, from tiny throwing stars to the long-range ice ray Nathan had wanted a go on since he'd first seen it. Blackthorn hesitated for a moment, deep in thought. *Now.*

"Hey, Blackthorn!" cried Nathan, leaping from the shadows. He raised his wrist and fired. Even Blackthorn didn't move fast enough this time. The bright green stasis ray froze the history teacher – or was it the RUIN mole? – to the spot. "Who's in detention now, huh?" asked Nathan. Blackthorn struggled against the stasis field, but it was no use. His face grew red. Nathan ran for the corridor, slamming buttons on the console and locking the history-teacher-spy-agent-mole in the armoury.

"Let's go."

One turn before the Central Server Room, they came to a stop. Zara peeked around the corner. Clear. They huddled around Screens.

"OK." Zara said, pointing to the screen. "RUIN will be here any moment. Talk to me: what's the plan?"

"I've got a black belt in Brazilian Jiu-Jitsu," said Kicks. "I'll just, erm... use it on all the ninjas?"

"It's a good start," said Zara. "Nathan, you help him. He'll need you and Zero. Keep them off me, and I'll make a run for the server room, swap the sticks, and we get out of here."

"OK." Screens pulled a bright blue memory stick from the laptop. "This has the key code for the Central Server Room door. You can't get in without it." She tossed the blue stick to Zara,

who caught it one-handed.

"Now this one," said Screens, showing Zara another memory stick, this time red, "has the fake list. You can swap them over once you're through the door. Got it?"

"Blue stick for the door. Dummy list on the red. Got it," Zara said, smiling at Screens. "Good work."

Nathan counted the ninjas between him and the door. Fourteen, fifteen…

"Sir," said Zero. "Your heart rate is very high and your stomach is rumbling at a rate of 0.3 gurgles per second. You are nervous, sir."

"I mean, there's a lot at stake here, Zero."

"Indeed, sir. Are you ready, sir?

"No," said Nathan. "But that's never stopped me before. Ready the stasis ray."

Zero vibrated and warmed up slightly. "Standard, or Full Blast, sir?"

Nathan narrowed his eyes at the RUIN ninjas. "Full Blast."

Yelling as loud as they could, Nathan and Kicks rushed forwards, followed by Zara. Kicks sent ninja after ninja flying, as Nathan and Zero froze the rest to the spot. Zara inched forwards,

dodging the green stasis ray and the whirling fists of a very excited Kicks.

"Take that!" Kicks yelled, kicking another ninja into the air. "And THAT! HA!"

The last three ninjas were the biggest, and they stood between the recruits and the door. Nathan and Zero took out the first, freezing the ninja in mid-air. Kicks spun, legs flying, and the second ninja flew down the corridor. Nathan ran, tucked and rolled, freezing the last ninja just

above him. "Zara, now!" he called. "Run!"

He looked over to see Zara... shaking hands with a RUIN agent? But...

WHAT?

"Zara! You're the mole!?" Nathan's heart sank into his shoes. Not ZARA?

"I love it when a plan goes exactly to plan." Zara laughed. "My plan!"

Nathan was too stunned to speak.

"RUIN thanks you for your service, Nathan Chase." Zara headed for the open Server Room door, tossing a small, black object behind her...

CHAPTER SIX
THE DISTANCE BETWEEN US

"Well, sir," said Zero. "We are, to use your mother's phrase, in a pickle."

"Stop quoting my mum in emergencies, Zero," said Nathan.

"Your mother gives very good advice," said Zero. "You should listen to her."

To Nathan's left, RUIN ninjas filled the doorway, fighting with each other to get in. To his right, a massive hole stood between Nathan and the server room… and Zara. Kicks ran in front of him, dealing smartly with the ninjas and only using maybe three of his black belts. Behind him, Screens tapped frantically.

"I can't shut it down!" she said. "I can't stop her, Nathan."

"Zero – how big is the gap?" Nathan raised his wrist and Zero scanned.

"Six metres seven centimetres, sir."

Well, that sounded… no, hang on. Jack Masters' voice rang in his head. They don't call Zero an artificial intelligence for nothing.

"Zero: suggestions, please?"

"Learning opportunity identified," said Zero.

"What did Agent Masters say this morning?"

Ahh. Nathan knew what to do.

"Screens – make me another copy of the fake." Nathan eyed the jump as Screens slid a yellow memory stick into the laptop and clicked furiously.

"OK, Zara," said Nathan. "Time to close the distance between us." He sprinted towards the hole. Screens tossed the yellow stick to him and he swiped it from the air, building speed.... and....

"Zero, NANO-STEP!" he cried. The cloud of

nano-bots formed under his foot. He pushed his weight down, then sprang from the step over the hole.

"Zero, CANCEL!" he cried. The step melted away. For a moment, Nathan flew upwards. He had to be in the air just long enough to –

"Zero, NANO-GRAPPLE!" he shouted. The bots flew upwards. Nathan felt gravity take control again. He reached –

His hand connected with the nano-rope as the hook thudded into the ceiling. Nathan swung, and as he reached the peak, launched over the hole, rolling to a stop at the door.

"Couldn't have done it without you," said Nathan.

Inside the server room, it was dark and hot. Bank after bank of computer towers filled the room. Each glass cabinet stood taller than Nathan, and red lights faded and glowed in complicated patterns. The soft whirr of fans deadened any sound. Quietly, Zero spoke.

"It's like we're in the brain of RADAR HQ." The screen glowed red as Zero took it all in. "It's **AMAZING**, sir."

Nathan couldn't believe Zara would betray them on purpose. RUIN must be forcing her to betray RADAR. Why else would she give up her training? Nathan wondered how they'd got to her. Well, it was OK. He'd found her first, and whatever it was, he would help his friend. He liked her too much to let her fall to RUIN.

At the end of the server room, with her back to Nathan, stood Zara, hunched over a console. She was fidgeting, clearly frustrated with something. As Nathan crept closer,

he could see the large screen in front of her. The blue memory stick stood up from a socket on the desk. On screen, a list of names scrolled and the desktop flashed with messages. **THE LIST: DOWNLOAD IN PROGRESS.** A wide bar crossed the centre of the screen, almost half filled with a glowing green, and above it read:

DOWNLOADING…43%

Zara was muttering under her breath.

"Stupid old… just use the cloud like everybody else… come on… come on…."

"Zara?" Nathan stepped forward and she whirled around.

"Go back, Nathan. Get out of here." She looked at the door. "There will be hundreds of RUIN ninjas here any moment."

"Kicks and Screens can handle it. I'm here for you. How did they make you do this?"

"What?" Confusion crossed her face, then her black lipstick curled into a strange, unfriendly smile. "Oh, Nathan. That's so SWEET. You think I'm being blackmailed by RUIN. That they've kidnapped my widdle kitten Fluffykins and won't give him back unless I betray RADAR. Don't you?" She laughed a horrible laugh.

"Not... not the bit about the cat. But... don't you need help?" Nathan frowned. What was she saying?

"They didn't MAKE me, Nathan. You really are useless without that watch. I'm NOT A RADAR STUDENT. I'm a RUIN agent. I have ALWAYS been the mole. I came here to take The List because I wanted to."

Nathan couldn't believe it. Zara... had been a RUIN agent all along. "You betrayed us?"

"Of course I did."
Zara smiled, almost sweetly. "My father asked me to." She replied. "And when your father is the head of RUIN, you tend to do what you're told."

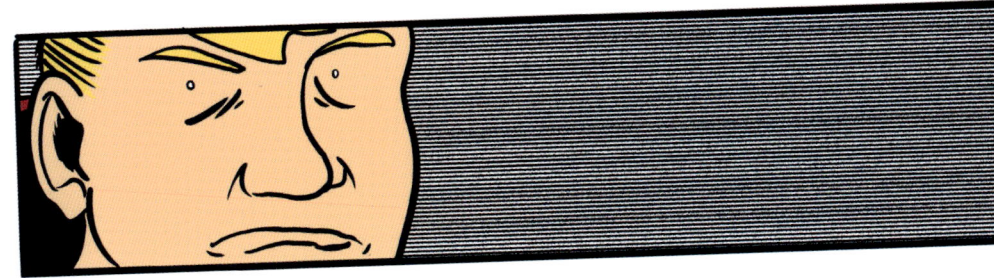

"Father?" But that meant... "Your DAD is... Baron von Thustra!"

CHAPTER SEVEN
THE YOU I THOUGHT I KNEW

"Don't you see the resemblance?" Zara laughed.

"I've never seen the Baron," said Nathan, still taking it all in.

Zero bleeped. "No one has ever seen the Baron, sir. We actually aren't even sure it's always the same person."

"Oh good, the watch is awake," said Zara.

"Ahem. I am not a watch. I am 0CT347-X. And you, madam —"

"Can call you Zero, I know," said Zara, rolling

her eyes.

"Actually," said Zero. "I was going to say: **YOU** are an agent of RUIN, and you are under arrest."

Zara laughed again. Her hand closed around the necklace at her throat, and she yanked hard on it, snapping the chain. She winked at Nathan. "Oh yeah?" she said. "What if I resist?" She squeezed the pendant and a stream of bright blue nano-bots beamed from the centre. They connected with a metallic shearing sound into the shimmering blade of a silver katana.

"Zero, can YOU do that?" asked Nathan in surprise.

"Yes, sir," replied Zero. Zara raised her sword. "And did I mention that I also make SHIELDS?!"

The nano-shield formed just as the katana smashed into it.

"There's still time to switch sides, Zara," Nathan cried.

Zara expertly swung the katana as if she'd been doing it since she was in nappies. "Why on Earth would I do that?"

"You don't have to follow your father. He's an evil man, Zara. Stay here; help us."

"I'm a von Thustra, Nathan." Zara swung low. Nathan leapt over the blade. Again, she came at him. Again, the nano-shield deflected the blow. "Evil kind of runs in the family."

"I don't care. You can choose your own path. Help us stop RUIN. You're not evil. I like you, Zara."

"Don't you mean 'liked'?" she spat.

"I said what I said." For a moment they stood, eye to eye, sword against shield.

"Stop this now, Zara." Nathan said. "This isn't the you I thought I knew."

"Stop this? Nathan Chase, I STARTED IT! I am Zara von Thustra. And that means only one thing: one day, I will rule the world!"

Nathan raised his shield just in time to stop the collapsing ceiling knocking him out. A RUIN flying saucer, round and silver, flashed and whirred above. Lightning flashed around its base. A metallic hum filled the air. A ladder fell and Zara, grabbing the memory stick from its dock on the console, leapt on. She rose through into the sky, waving the stick at Nathan. "RUIN thanks you for your help!" she shouted, blowing

Nathan a kiss before vanishing into the craft and racing away.

Nathan watched the saucer shrink from sight. Zero vibrated.

"Are you... smiling, sir?" said Zero.

Nathan straightened his face. Evil or not, Zara had been magnificent with that sword. "No."

"Sir, post-battle checks show your body temperature has gone up 0.93 degrees. Concentrated... in the face. Specifically: your cheeks. Are you... blushing, sir?"

Jack Masters and the others raced into the room. Nathan exhaled. Of course he wasn't blushing. Why would he be blushing?

"They got The List!" Jack cried.

Nathan, grateful for the change of subject, smiled. "No, they didn't."

"What do you mean?" said Foxley.

"What happened?" said Kicks.

"Why are you blushing?" said Screens.

"Shall we show them, Zero?" said Nathan.

"Affirmative, sir," said Zero.

Nathan opened his fist. In his palm nestled the blue memory stick.

"You got it!" cried Screens.

"What's going on?" said Kicks. "Isn't that the dummy list?"

"No, the second copy was yellow." Explained Screens. "Zara did download the real list to the blue stick..."

"But she took it?" Kicks looked confused. "We saw her waving it?"

"I switched the uploaded list with the yellow dummy when we were fighting." Nathan smiled and tossed the blue stick with the real list to Screens.

"And Princess Bad Guy flew off with the dummy!" Screens smiled and clicked the real list into the desktop. The names started rolling onto the screen.

"That was rather close, Masters," said Foxley. "Too close. RUIN agents were inside RADAR HQ!"

"What was Zara's talent?" asked Kicks, frowning. "She doesn't have any black belts. She's rubbish with computers. How did she get recruited?"

"Zara Thornberry, as we thought she was called, was recruited because she's a world-class expert in... well, in deception," said Foxley.

"She's a receptionist?" Kicks looked confused.

"She's a MASSIVE LIAR." Said Screens. "Obviously."

"She sure fooled us." Jack Masters shook his head.

"Jack?" asked Nathan. "Why did you recruit

me?"

"Actually," said Jack, putting an arm around Nathan's shoulder. "You remind me of someone. The best agent I ever knew. I saw it in your eye – I just knew you would get the job done."

Nathan smiled. He knew where he belonged.

EPILOGUE
RUIN HQ
LOCATION: UNKNOWN

There is a place that is so secret and so spooky that only the most senior RUIN agents have ever been there. A thousand miles of black forest stretches as far as the eye can see, in every direction. The skies are always dark, the clouds are always low, and the air is filled with huge solemn birds like broken, black umbrellas, flapping across the sky.

Lightning flashes and in its glare, you can catch a glimpse of a terrible place. A high, dark castle sits on the edge of a tall, dark cliff. Jagged rocks line the castle walls. To even reach the gates, The Way of Ten Thousand Steps must be travelled on foot. Ten thousand narrow, slippery steps, carved into the wet rock of the cliff face, stand between any mortal person and the sacred lair of Baron von Thustra. All the way, the squawking birds peck at your clothes, and lightning flashes overhead. Most never make it to the top.

If, however, you are the daughter of the Baron, you arrive in style.

Zara's flying saucer glided to a stop on the parapets. She stepped from the craft and a crew of ninjas carried her things into the castle. She walked into her suite of rooms, past deep purple drapes, and long, grand flags bearing the emblem of RUIN. The thick heels of her heavy boots clicked against the cold, hard floors. She breathed in the damp, cool air, and smiled. It was good to be home. And Daddy was going to be so pleased with her this time.

At her father's door, she hesitated. Squeezing the memory stick in her palm, she took a deep breath, then nodded at the ninjas waiting by each door. They flung them open and she strode through.

The shadows in the throne room were the deepest in the whole castle, and her father's looming presence could be felt in the air. Despite herself, she shivered.

"ZARA," he boomed from the shadows. His

voice was low, and rasped with metallic tones. His breath, through his mask, was deep and harsh. At the back of the room, a bank of computers glowed ominously. The enormous, hulking shadow of Baron von Thustra crossed the screens, the faint light gleaming off his armour, and Zara could see her father properly for the first time, hidden as always behind his purple mask. His eyes in the sockets glowed faintly. She dropped to her knees on the floor, bowed her head, and offered up the yellow memory stick.

"The List, Father. Just as you asked."

The baron reached out and plucked the stick from her with his gloved hand. The thorny metal claws he wore over his exoskin scratched lightly at Zara's palm, leaving a faint red mark. He whirled around, a cold breeze sweeping over her as the back of his cloak brushed her knees. The baron held out the stick and immediately a ninja appeared from the shadows, took it, and inserted it into the slot on the consoles behind him. Zara, on the floor behind her father, watched his back as he watched the screen.

The console lit up, casting her father into a solid black shadow. The ninja at the controls clicked and Zara watched as a list of names filled the screen. Her father turned and looked at her.

"Acceptable," he intoned deeply.

He had never said anything so nice to her. Zara looked up, her eyes full of hope and tears. Behind her father, the files on screen started to slow down and the names became visible.

Commander Arthur C. Foxley

Agent Jack Masters

Agent Al A. Gator

Agent Anita Bath

Agent Chris P. Bacon

Wait a minute. Chris... P.... Oh no.

Something was wrong. Her face fell. His breath through the mask was short and tight.

"Nathan Chase, what did you do?" she breathed.

Agent Mick. E Mouse

Agent Dinah Mite

Agent Don Key

Across the screen, bright red letters were starting to form. Zara was already running for the door before they had finished. The baron, roaring with rage, thumped his fists into the console. Above his head, across the screen in nine-inch letters it read:

RUIN SUCKS!

MISSION LOG
NATHAN CHASE

...and so, the invasion of RADAR HQ failed. But it was a close call. Too close. Foxley was yelling for hours about how the Baron's actual daughter managed to dupe us all. But I know Zara. I know deep down she isn't bad.

I've got to go back to civilian school on Monday. Foxley says I have to "lay low" for a little bit while RADAR works out what's next. It's not too bad — at least I've got the school trip to see Barry Thunder to look forward to. I can't wait to go to the museum — I've always wanted to see a real T-rex, even if it is just a fossil.

I just hope I can get to Zara before the other agents do. I know she can be saved, but I don't know if the others will give her a chance. I know she's amazing. I already miss her — class is kind of quiet now. Anyway, by the time they found Blackthorn (who, it turned out, was not the mole – who knew?) he was in a very, VERY bad mood with me, so I have to do RADAR detention for a million Saturday afternoons now. I've got plenty of time to think about what to do next, I suppose.

Kicks, Screens and I are getting along great, though. Turns out, we're a good team. Even if I don't quite know what is special about me yet, I'm still learning loads. And now there are some people I can call my friends at least. I know they've got my back in a pickle, as Mum would say.

My head is full of questions. How can I help Zara get away from her father – and does she even want to? How can I get Blackthorn to stop hating me long enough to actually read my homework? And will I get to meet Barry Thunder on the school trip? I don't know what's coming next but, since RADAR entered my life, I know it won't be boring!

Agent Nathan Chase: OUT